The Titanic is Sinking

LONGMAN

Addison Wesley Longman Limited
Edinburgh Gate, Harlow
Essex CM20 2JE, England
and Associated Companies throughout the world.

© K R Cripwell 1979

First published by Collins ELT 1979

This edition published by Addison Wesley Longman Ltd 1995
Fifth impression 1998

ISBN 0-17-556580-5

Design by Shireen Nathoo Design

Cover illustration by Archer Quinnell / Début Art

The publishers would like to thank the following for permission to use photographs:
The Hulton Picture Company, p21 (bottom left), p22-23, p24, p25; Popperfoto, p20 (top right), p20 (bottom), p21 (bottom right); Topham Picture Source, p20 (top left), p21 (top).

All Rights Reserved. This publication is protected in the United Kingdom by the Copyright Act 1988 and in other countries by comparable legislation. No part of it may be reproduced or recorded by any means without the permission of the publisher. This prohibition extends (with certain very limited exceptions) to photocopying and similar processes, and written permission to make a copy or copies must therefore be obtained from the publisher in advance. It is advisable to consult the publisher if there is any doubt regarding the legality of any proposed copying.

Printed in Malaysia, PP

Contents

1 A Good Start 5
2 The Iceberg 9
3 You Cannot Sink this Ship 13
4 Women and Children First 18
5 A Time to Say Goodbye 28
6 Maybe the Sea Knows the Answers 32
  Exercises 37
  Glossary 46

1
A Good Start

The year was 1907. Dinner was over. 'Come, Mrs Ismay. Let's leave the men to their drinks. I know what they're going to talk about. Ships! But I don't like to talk about ships. I only like going on ships. Don't you?'

'You're so right, Lady Pirrie. My husband is always talking about ships. He only thinks of ships. He sees ships in his sleep.' Mrs Ismay laughed and looked at her husband with a smile. 'But he is the head of the White Star Line.'

'And the White Star Line is the greatest shipping line in the world,' said Lord Pirrie. 'That's where I come in. I'm the head of Harland and Wolff. We build ships. And I want to build some new ships for your husband.'

'Make them pretty ships,' said Lady Pirrie, as she opened the door into the next room. 'Make them with beautiful rooms. Big rooms where you can dance. Lovely bedrooms and lots of bathrooms. Build a ship that's beautiful like this house.'

'And strong,' said Mrs Ismay. 'I never liked the sea

very much. I wouldn't like sea water in my house.' She gave another laugh and closed the door behind her.

'Can we give them all that, Pirrie?' said Ismay.

'Of course we can,' answered Lord Pirrie.

'Why don't you build me three ships?' said Ismay. 'I want them to be the biggest passenger ships in the world. Maybe not the fastest. But they must be just like this house. They must be a home from home for the richest of rich passengers. They must also carry the most passengers. I want to carry the rich and famous people of the world. But I must carry poor passengers too. I want to carry all the poor people of Europe in my ships. In America they'll become rich and they'll remember my ships.'

'Let me get some paper,' said Lord Pirrie. He took some paper and a pencil from an inside pocket. 'Is this the kind of thing you want?' He began to draw on the paper.

'Yes, I think that's right.'

'Good. I'll start work on it in the morning. But let's go back and see our wives now. They must think that we're asleep,' said Lord Pirrie with a laugh. The two men got up and went to the room next door.

Soon work began on the first two ships. The name of the first ship was the *Olympic*. The name of the second was the *Titanic*. The *Titanic* was bigger than the *Olympic*. She was the biggest ship in the world. The newspapers said she was bigger than the Washington Memorial. And two times longer than St Peter's in Rome and the Grand Pyramid together.

Only the best was good enough for the *Titanic*. The most expensive beds and baths. The most expensive knives and forks. The most expensive tables.

'We must have gold plates in the best dining room,' said a man at one meeting.

'Who wants gold plates?' said another person. 'People will only try to take them home with them.'

There was a lot of laughter round the table.

'I think white plates with a gold line will be pretty, don't you? Too much gold looks bad, don't you think?' said another.

They talked for hours. Then one man said, 'We must talk about the lifeboats.'

But the meeting did not want to talk about the lifeboats. They wanted to talk about beautiful things. Then after four or five hours they did talk about the lifeboats.

'Are there enough lifeboats?' asked one man.

'Yes.'

'Where will they be?'

'On top.'

There were a few more questions. They talked about the lifeboats for only ten minutes.

Harland and Wolff built both the *Olympic* and the

Titanic in Belfast. They built them on land first. Then on 31 May 1911 the *Titanic* was ready for the sea. She took 62 seconds to move from land into the water.

Harland and Wolff took another year to finish her. She left Belfast on 2 April 1912. They tried her both fast and slow. They tried her kitchens. All went well. She was ready for her passengers.

She left Southampton for New York on Wednesday 10 April. She stopped at Cherbourg in France for more passengers. She arrived at Queenstown in Ireland on 11 April about midday. Most of the new passengers were poor Irish people. They were going to America for jobs.

Then the *Titanic* was on her way across the Atlantic. The most expensive, the biggest and the most beautiful ship in the world.

2

The Iceberg

High up in the ship, Frederick Fleet looked into the night. There was no moon but the stars were bright. The sea was still. It was very cold. It was the fifth night of the *Titanic's* first crossing of the Atlantic.

The *Titanic* had six men who were lookouts. These men were the eyes of the ship. Fleet remembered the words of one of his officers: 'Look out for icebergs. We've heard that there are some about.'

It was 10 o'clock at night. Fleet could see nothing dangerous in front of the ship. He spoke to the other lookout, Reginald Lee. 'I'm so cold,' he said. 'I can see nothing. Can you?'

'No. I've never seen the sea still and quiet like this.'

'And we're going fast now, aren't we?'

Now it was 11.40 p.m. on Sunday 14 April. Only twenty minutes to midnight.

Suddenly Fleet saw something in front of him. It was small but every minute it grew bigger and bigger. He took up the telephone and spoke to the officer on the bridge of the ship.

'What do you see?'

'An iceberg in front of the ship,' said Fleet.

'Thank you,' said the officer.

For the next half a minute Lee and Fleet looked at the iceberg. It came nearer and nearer. Still the ship did not turn. 'We're going to hit it if we don't turn soon,' thought Fleet. The iceberg was higher than the *Titanic*. It was green in the light of the stars. The two lookouts felt the touch of the iceberg. But it was not a big bang.

Down below other people felt something. Nobody thought that it was dangerous. But some passengers saw the iceberg as it passed their windows.

Some young men felt the bang and went outside to look. They saw the iceberg. One man called out, 'We hit an iceberg – there it is.' The others said nothing. But the iceberg passed and the ship went on.

'Let's go in,' said one man, 'and have another drink. I can't see it. It's too dark. Nothing's happened.'

But he was wrong.

Just then Captain Smith came onto the bridge. 'Mr Murdoch, what was that?' he asked.

'An iceberg, sir. I turned the ship and I've now stopped her. I tried to go round the iceberg but she was too close. I couldn't do any more.'

'Close the emergency doors.'

'The doors are already closed.'

Down below Fred Barrett saw the red lights. Then he saw the water. 'Water's coming in,' he said. He ran through the emergency doors. Just in time! The emergency doors closed behind him. But on the other side of the emergency doors things were no better.

'Help! Help!'
'The sea's coming in!'
'We've hit an iceberg!'
'We've hit Newfoundland!'
'Help! Help me ...'

The red lights went on and off. Men ran from one place to another.

About 15 kilometres away Third Officer Charles Groves stood on the bridge of the *Californian*. She was on her way from London to Boston. She was a small ship. She was still because of all the dangerous icebergs. A big ship with lots of lights passed the *Californian*.

'Do they know about the icebergs?' Groves thought. 'They're going very fast. I think I'll tell the captain.'

Captain Lord said, 'Tell them about the icebergs. Use the lamp.'

Groves started to do this. Suddenly all the lights on the big ship went out. 'Many ships do that,' thought Groves, 'to send the passengers to bed early.' He laughed.

'They'll soon be in New York.'

It was the *Titanic*. The lights had not gone out. When she turned Groves could see only the back of the ship. There were no lights there. And the men on the bridge of the *Titanic* did not see Groves's lamp. They did not know that another ship was close. And Groves did not know that the *Titanic* was no longer on its way to New York. He put the lamp away. His work was over for the night. Two other officers, Stone and Gibson, took his place on the bridge.

3

You Cannot Sink this Ship

'Why have we stopped?'

'I don't know, sir. There's talk of an iceberg. We've stopped to let it go by. It's not dangerous.'

All over the ship passengers asked the same question. Most went back to bed. But some of the passengers in the bottom of the ship did not. Carl Johnson heard the bang and got out of bed. His feet touched the floor and he felt cold water. He put his clothes on fast. As he left his room the water was already over his shoes.

The cold sea water soon filled the lower parts of the ship. The lights went off and the sailors could not see in the dark.

'Put out the fires!'

'Leave at once!'

'Quick! Quick! Get out now!'

On the bridge Captain Smith heard the news. It was bad. 'The water's coming in fast,' said one officer. 'It's filling the lower part of the ship.'

Just then Bruce Ismay arrived on the bridge.
'What's happened?' he asked.
'We've hit an iceberg,' said Captain Smith.
'It's made a hole in the ship below the water.'
'Is it dangerous?'
'Yes, I'm afraid it is.'
'Send for Andrews. He's the builder of the ship,' said Ismay. 'He built this ship. He must know more about her than any of us.'

Thomas Andrews and Captain Smith went below together. They saw the water. They listened to the ship's officers and men. They went back to the bridge. Their faces did not show what they felt.

Suddenly the ship moved.
'What's that?' said one passenger to another. 'The sea is still and the boat has stopped. Did you feel it?'
The other passenger said nothing.
'The front of the ship is getting lower. Can't you feel it?'
'Oh, I don't know. You cannot sink this boat.'
On the bridge the Captain said to Thomas Andrews, 'You're the builder. What do you think?'
'There's a hole about 100 metres long below the water. There's water in five of the sixteen compartments.'
'Well, what does that mean?' asked Ismay.

'It means this,' said Andrews. 'The *Titanic* is made of sixteen compartments. Each compartment is like a very strong box. We can close any of the compartments. The doors between the compartments are very strong. So if there is a hole in one compartment we can close it with the emergency doors. Then the water cannot get into the next compartment.'

'We've done that,' said Captain Smith.

'With water in one compartment the *Titanic* can't sink. Of course, it would be dangerous but the ship will not sink. With water in two compartments the ship will not sink. With water in three or four of the compartments the ship will not sink. But if five of the sixteen compartments have water in them the front of the ship will sink into the water. When that happens water from the fifth compartment will get into the sixth compartment.'

'And then ...?' said Ismay.

'Water will fill all the compartments one by one. And the ship will sink.'

'Is there no way to save the ship?'

'I'm afraid not.'

At 12.05 a.m. the Captain said, 'Get the boats ready. Tell the passengers. The ship is sinking.' It was twenty-five minutes after the bang.

Then Captain Smith walked towards the radio room. John Phillips, the radio officer, was very tired. The job of a radio officer was very hard at that time. Radio was new and it was not very strong. Passengers enjoyed the radio. They sent lots of messages to all their friends. John Phillips sent the messages by radio to Cape Race in America. From Cape Race they went to all parts of the world.

At 11.55 Second Radio Officer Bride spoke to Phillips. 'Are you tired, John? Let me take your place now. I've had a good sleep.'

'Thanks, I've just finished with Cape Race. It's been a bad night. I haven't stopped all day. I've had more messages than ever. About an hour ago I spoke to Cape Race. The sound was strong. Then in the middle of my message I heard from another ship: the *Californian*. She was very close. I said, "Shut up! Shut up! Can't you hear I'm talking to Cape Race?"'

'What did the *Californian* say?'

'Something about icebergs.'

'Nothing else?'

'Nothing.'

Bride took Phillips' place. Phillips changed and got into bed. Just then the Captain came into the radio room.

'We've hit an iceberg,' he said to Bride. 'Get ready to send out a call for help. But don't send it until I tell you.'

He left, but in a few minutes he was back. 'Send the call for help now,' he said.

By this time Phillips was back at the radio. At 12.15

he started to send the call for help. 'CQD MGY CQD MGY CQD MGY CQD MGY CQD MGY ...' At that time CQD was the call for help. MGY was the call letters for the *Titanic*. He sent the call six times.

On the *Californian* fifteen kilometres away Charles Groves was in the radio room.

'Have you closed for the night?' he asked the Radio Officer, Cyril Evans.

'Yes. I closed at 11.30. I've finished for today. It's been a bad night.'

'What ships have you spoken to?'

'Only the *Titanic*. And they told me to shut up.'

Groves listened to the radio for a moment. He could hear nothing. He left the radio room at 12.15 and went to bed.

4

Women and Children First

'The ship is sinking. Put on your life-jackets. Get ready to leave the ship.'

All the people on the *Titanic* soon heard the news. Passengers left their rooms. Some put coats over their night clothes. Some took a few oranges and left boxes of money. Some took a book to read. They made little noise as they went above. The first class passengers stood together in the centre of the ship. The second class passengers stood further back and the third class stood at the back of the ship.

The sailors started to get the lifeboats ready. There were sixteen boats: eight on each side. Four were near the front. And four were nearer the back of the ship. They were all made of wood. There were also four boats made of cloth.

All the boats together could carry 1178 people. There were 2207 people on the *Titanic*.

But the passengers were not afraid. They still did not believe that the end of the *Titanic* was near.

'The *Titanic* cannot sink! She's the biggest ship in the world! The Captain and his men know their jobs,' they thought. 'They'll save us.'

But this was the first time for the sailors and their officers. So the work was slow.

'Let down Boat Number 4,' said one officer.

'No wait,' said another. 'We're not ready.'

'The captain says so.'

'All right.'

'Fill her up.'

'Not yet.'

'Why not? The captain says so. Women and children first.'

Then a few minutes later: 'What's wrong now?'

'The windows are closed. Nobody can get out.'

'Well, open the windows. Break them but get the passengers into the boats.'

But the women and children did not want to get into the boats.

'Things are better here than in that little boat,' said one.

'Come on, miss,' said a sailor to an old woman.

'I won't go,' she answered.

'Let her stay if she won't get in,' said an officer to the

sailor. 'But fill the boat.'

Very few women and children got into the boats. So the officers began to ask for husbands and wives together.

Then a few men.

The boats began to fill slowly. When there were 18 passengers in Boat Number 4 the officer said, 'Let it down.'

It was the first boat in the water.

'How long have we got?' Captain Smith asked Andrews.

'About an hour, I think,' he said. 'The water's coming in fast.'

In the radio room John Phillips sent his call for help again and again. The first reply was from the *Frankfort* at 12.18. Then he heard from the *Mount Temple*, the *Virginian* and the *Birma*. The air was soon full of talk. Too much talk.

'Do you know that Cape Race wants you?' said the radio officer of the *Carpathia*.

'Come at once,' John Phillips answered. 'We've hit an iceberg. It's CQD, old man. We are 41.46 North, 50.14 West.'

'Shall I tell the captain?' asked the *Carpathia*.

'Yes, quick.'

A few minutes later the *Carpathia's* radio officer said, 'We're coming. We're seventy kilometres from you.'

'This is the *Frankfort*.'

'Where are you?'

'We're 240 kilometres from you.'

'Are you coming to help? Tell your captain. We are on the ice.'

'What call are you using?' Bride asked John Phillips, later.

'CQD,' Phillips answered.

'Why not use the new call – SOS? It's much easier.'

So John Phillips began to use the new call SOS – dot-dot-dot-dash-dash-dash-dot-dot-dot. It was now 12.45.

But what about the *Californian*? It was only 15 kilometres away. The officers on the bridge of the *Titanic* could see its lights. One officer tried to send a message with a lamp. But there was no reply. Captain Smith said, 'Send up some rockets. They must come to our help.'

One of the officers on the bridge of the *Californian* saw a rocket in the sky.

'That's strange,' he said. 'Why have they sent up a rocket? They must be having a good time. I've tried to send a message about the icebergs. But they don't answer. I did see a light from them once or twice. But I don't think that it was a message. Some people do strange things at sea. Rockets!'

Captain E J Smith
of the Titanic

The Titanic leaving Queenstown Harbour
after taking on the mail

The last message received from the ship after she had struck a
submerged iceberg

*Drawings made by a survivor, on an overturned collapsible boat,
as the Titanic was sinking*

*The news on
the 15th April 1912*

*Survivors from the Titanic arriving
alongside the Carpath*

The Titanic disappearing beneath the waves – an artists impression

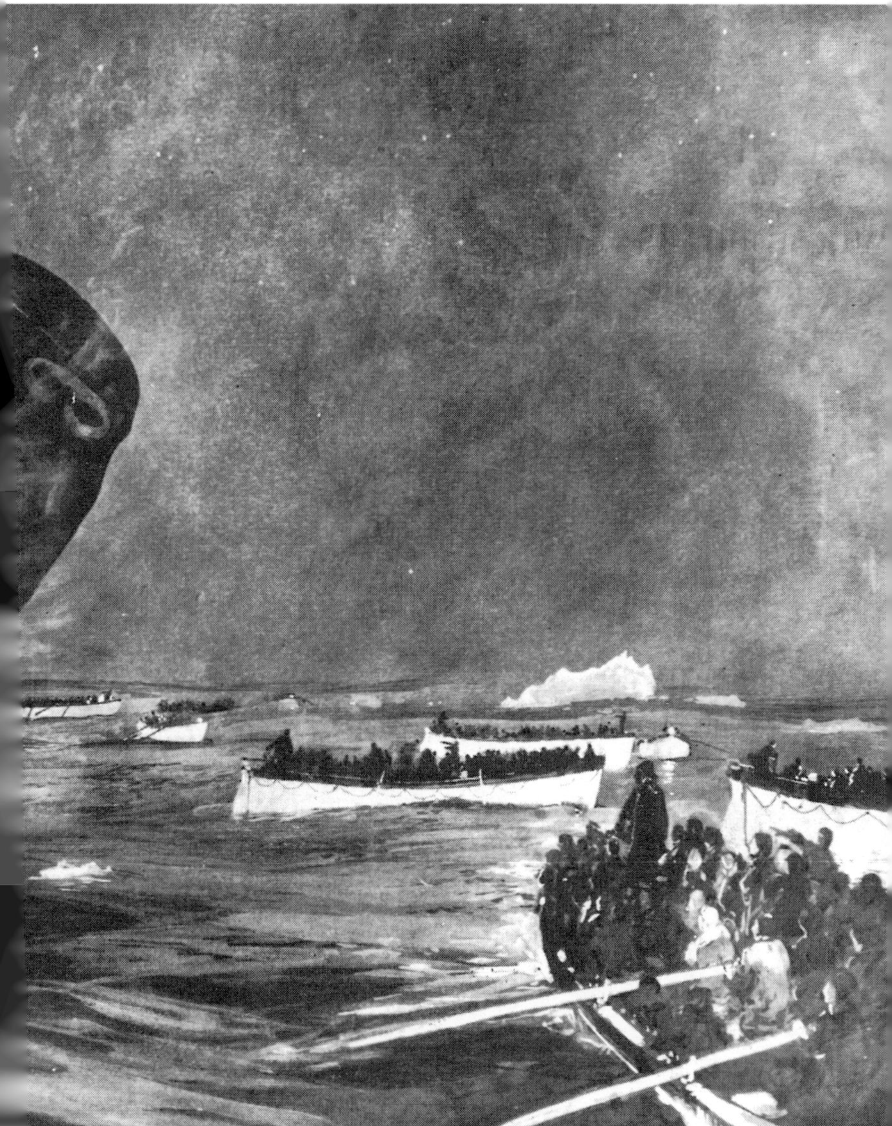

THE BRIEF CAREER OF THE LARGEST LINER
DESCRIBED IN THREE TABLEAUX

DEPARTURE —THE LEVIATHAN (AND HER COMMANDER, CAPTAIN SMITH) LEAVING SOUTHAMPTON— APRIL 10

DOOM —THE FATE OF THE TITANIC, ILLUSTRATED BY ICEBERGS FLOATING IN THE ATLANTIC— APRIL 14, 10.25 P.M.

DISTRESS —SCENES AT THE WHITE STAR OFFICES IN COCKSPUR STREET AND THE CITY— APRIL 15

The Titanic's first and last voyage was ill-fated from the very first, for as she was leaving Southampton the displacement of so much water caused the New York to break away from the quayside, and a collision nearly resulted. Her commander, Captain E. J. Smith, R.N., who is reported to have gone down with the liner, was captain of the Olympic when, last September, she collided with the cruiser Hawke off the Isle of Wight. Two of our pictures show a battleship in peril amid icebergs, which are submerged to the extent of seven-eighths of their bulk.

*The last days of the Titanic –
the events of April 10-15, 1914*

Survivors of the Titanic disaster

5

A Time to Say Goodbye

The passengers also saw the rockets.

'That means that things are bad,' said one passenger to his young wife. 'They don't send up rockets for nothing. We'd better say goodbye now.'

'It's all right, little girl,' said Dan Marvin to his new wife.

'You go and I'll stay a while.'

'I'll see you later,' said Adolf Hyker as he helped his wife into a boat.

Mark Fortune and his son helped his wife and three daughters into a boat. 'We're going in the next boat,' he said.

'Charles, help father,' one of the girls called to her brother.

'Walter,' said Mrs Douglas, 'You must come with me.'

'No,' he answered. 'I must be a man.'

'Then try to go with Major Butt and Mr Moore,' his wife said. 'They're big, strong men.'

'Women and children first.' Now nobody wanted to stay behind on the *Titanic*. The front of the ship was deeper in the water now. Thomas Andrews walked among the passengers. 'You *must* get in at once,' he said. 'There's not a minute to lose. Get in! Get in!'

One after another the lifeboats dropped into the sea.

One old woman cried out, 'Don't put me in the boat. I don't want to go in the boat. I've never been in an open boat before.'

'You must go,' said an officer.

Most people went quietly. Some of the passengers could not speak English. They could not understand the officers and the officers could not understand them. Many of the third class passengers became afraid. Some got into boats but many did not. They ran from one place to another. They asked questions and did not wait for answers.

Most of the boats were now gone. One by one they left the side of the *Titanic*. From the boats all eyes were on the ship. They could see the people. They could see the lights. And they could hear the music of the ship's band. It was happy dance music.

Captain Smith said to the sailors in Boat 8, 'Can you see the lights of that ship over there? Take your passengers to it. Then come back for more.'

Then he said to an officer, 'Can you send a message to that ship?'

'Yes, sir.'

'Tell her this. "We are the *Titanic*. We're sinking. Please have all your boats ready."'

Again and again the officers tried to call the ship. But they got no answer. They sent up more rockets. Someone must see their calls for help.

On the *Californian* two officers, Stone and Gibson, counted the rockets. They saw five rockets. Gibson sent a message with his lamp. At one o'clock he saw a sixth rocket.

At 1.10 Stone spoke to the captain of the *Californian*, Captain Lord, on the telephone. He told him about the six rockets. 'I don't know what they mean, sir,' he said. 'What shall I do?'

'Send another message with your lamp,' the captain said.

Stone and Gibson on the bridge could see the ship through their glasses. 'Have a look at her now,' Gibson said. 'She looks very strange. One side is very high out of the water. Now her red lights have gone out.'

The sea was over the front of the ship. Now *all* the passengers wanted to escape in the lifeboats. One young Irishman, David Buckley, jumped into a boat with some other men. He put a cloth over his head. He looked like a young woman. So an officer let him stay. But the other men had to leave.

Another young man tried to hide in a boat. An officer found him 'You must wait. Women and children first.'

The young man began to cry. So the officer took out a gun. The boy cried louder. 'Be a man,' said the officer. He took the boy by an arm. All the women and children in the boat started to cry. One girl said, 'Oh, Mr Man, don't shoot, please don't shoot the poor young man.'

The boy left quietly.

Then a crowd of men tried to get into the boat. The officer took out his gun again. 'Don't try to get in this boat or I'll use this.' he said. He shot three times into the sea.

'Stand back! Stand back! It's women first!'

One by one the lifeboats dropped into the sea. At last there was only one wooden lifeboat left. By then the sea was only five metres below it.

There were forty-seven seats in the last lifeboat. There were 1600 people still on the *Titanic*. Sailors held the crowds away from the boat. 'Women and children only,' said an officer.

A father brought two baby boys. 'Take them,' he said. Then he went back into the crowd.

Mr Harris brought his wife forward. 'Yes, I know,' he said to the officers. 'I will stay.'

Miss Evans gave her place to a married woman. 'You go first,' she said. 'You have children at home.'

6

Maybe the Sea Knows the Answers

There were no more lifeboats. Only two cloth boats were left. But nobody could get them free. All those on the *Titanic* knew that the end was near. All was still and quiet. Only the band played on. It was slow dance music.

John Phillips in the radio room still sat at his radio. Second Radio Officer Bride stood near him. Captain Smith came inside the radio room.

'Men,' he said, 'you can do no more.'

But Phillips did not stop.

Men began to jump into the cold sea. Some swam to the lifeboats. But most of the officers and sailors stayed on the ship. They waited quietly or walked up and down. Most people tried to get to the back of the ship. This was now high out of the water.

On the bridge Captain Smith remembered the four messages about icebergs from the day before. He thought about the cold water.

John Phillips remembered the message about icebergs from the *Californian* at 11 o'clock.

Everyone remembered little things from the past. But it was now too late.

At 2.10 John Phillips was still at the radio. Bride came into the room. A sailor was behind Phillips. 'Look out,' cried Bride. 'He's taking your life-jacket.'

Bride jumped on the man and Phillips hit him a number of times. The sailor fell to the floor. 'Come on,' cried Bride. 'The sea's at the door.'

The two men ran outside. The sailor lay still on the floor.

There was no more dance music. The band began to play 'Autumn'.

The people in the lifeboats could hear the music. The men on the ship didn't listen to the music: the end was too near.

'Oh, save me! Save me,' a young woman cried.

'Only God can save you now,' said a young man. But he took her arm and together they jumped over the side.

The front of the boat began to go down fast. Water soon filled it. Then the back of the ship began to come up out of the water. Then it began to go down too. The lights were still on. Only the back of the ship was above water.

There was a number of very loud bangs. Then the noise stopped.

'That's the last of her.'

'She's gone.'

Third Officer Pitman in one of the boats looked at his watch. 'It's 2.20,' he said.

Fifteen kilometres away Stone and Gibson on the *Californian* looked at the *Titanic* through their glasses. At 2.05 Stone spoke to Captain Lord on the telephone. 'The ship has sent off eight rockets. She is very low in the water.'

'Were they all white rockets?' the captain asked.

'Yes,' replied Stone.

'What's the time?' Captain Lord asked.

'2.05, sir.'

Captain Lord then went back to sleep.

At 2.20 Stone said to Gibson, 'It's gone.'

Then at 2.40 he again tried to speak to the captain. But the captain was asleep.

At 4.00 Chief Officer George Stewart took the place of Stone on the bridge of the *Californian*. Stone told him about the rockets. He told him of another rocket from the south at 3.40. 'All the others were to the north,' he said. Then he went to bed.

At 4.30 Stewart spoke to the captain about the last rocket.

'Yes, I know,' said Captain Lord. 'I'm coming up to the bridge now.'

'Shall we send a message?' asked Stewart.

'No, I don't think so.'

At 5.40 Stewart woke Radio Officer Evans. He told him about the rockets in the night. 'Find out what's happened,' he said.

Two minutes later Evans ran up to Stewart. His face was white. 'A ship's sunk,' he said. 'The *Titanic* has hit an iceberg and sunk.'

Captain Lord jumped up. 'Quick,' he said. 'Get this ship there now. We must help if we can.'

1502 people went down with the *Titanic*. Most of these were poor people from the third class.

What went wrong?

There were not enough lifeboats.

The radio was too weak. There were too many messages on the radio. The radio officers finished work at 11.30 in those days.

Icebergs are *very* dangerous and nobody knew enough about them.

Today all ships must carry enough lifeboats for all the people on the ship. Ship radios must work 24 hours a day. All ships must listen to the radio for news about icebergs.

Why didn't the *Californian* go to help the *Titanic* in time?

What happened to Captain Smith?

Nobody knows. Like many other questions about the *Titanic*, nobody knows.

Maybe the sea knows one or two of the answers.

Exercises

A Comprehension

CHAPTER 1

Try to remember. Then check your answers.
1 What did Mrs Ismay say her husband saw in his sleep?
2 What did Lord Pirrie say he wanted to do for the White Star Line shipping company?
3 What were the names of the first two ships built by Harland and Wolff?
4 What did they talk about for only ten minutes at one meeting?
5 What country did the *Titanic* sail to before going to Ireland?

CHAPTER 2

Are these statements true or false? Check your answers.

		True	False
1	The *Titanic* had seven lookouts.	☐	☐
2	There was a big bang when the *Titanic* hit the iceberg.	☐	☐
3	Mr Murdoch waited for the captain to tell him to close the emergency doors before closing them.	☐	☐
4	The *Californian* was going from London to Boston.	☐	☐
5	Third Officer Groves thought the lights on the *Titanic* had been put out.	☐	☐

CHAPTER 3

Choose the correct answer, A, B or C. Then check your answers.

1. When Carl Johnson put his foot on the cabin floor, he felt...
   A ice
   B a lifejacket
   C sea water
2. Thomas Andrews knew all about the *Titanic* because he...
   A sailed the ship
   B worked the radio
   C built the ship
3. The hole in the *Titanic* was...
   A a hundred feet long
   B a hundred metres long
   C a mile long
4. The number of compartments that had to fill up with sea water before the *Titanic* sank was ...
   A five
   B four
   C two
5. At the time the *Titanic* sank the usual radio call for help was...
   A SOS
   B CQD
   C MGY
6. The call sign SOS means ...
   A sinking of ship
   B save our souls
   C save our ship

CHAPTER 4

Try to remember. Then check your answers.

1. All the lifeboats together could hold 1178 people. About how many people were there on the *Titanic*?
2. Why did the passengers say the *Titanic* could not sink?

EXERCISES

3 Why did the women and children not want to get into the lifeboats?
4 How long did the passengers have to get into the lifeboats before the *Titanic* sank?
5 The *Carpathia* was 70 kilometres away from the *Titanic* when they got the call for help. If the *Carpathia's* top speed was 20 kilometres an hour, could it have got there in time to help?
6 Why didn't the officers on the *Californian* help the *Titanic* when they saw the lights and rockets?

CHAPTER 5

Choose the correct answer, A, B or C. Then check your answers.

1 Some of the passengers didn't know what the officers were saying because...
   A they couldn't hear well
   B there was too much noise on the ship
   C they couldn't speak English
2 The passengers in the lifeboats could hear the ship's band playing...
   A church music
   B happy dance music
   C sad music
3 Captain Lord of the *Californian* told one of his officers to send a message to the *Titanic* by...
   A telephone
   B radio
   C (signal) lamp
4 To get into a lifeboat, David Buckley pretended he was a...
   A child
   B radio operator
   C young woman
5 Miss Evans gave up her place in the lifeboat to a...
   A single woman
   B married woman with children at home
   C married woman

CHAPTER 6

Are these statements true or false? Check your answers.

		True	False
1	All the lifeboats from the *Titanic* left the ship with passengers on them.	☐	☐
2	Most of the ship's officers and sailors stayed on board the sinking ship.	☐	☐
3	Most of the passengers who went down with the *Titanic* were travelling first class.	☐	☐
4	Everybody knew how dangerous icebergs were at the time when the *Titanic* sank.	☐	☐
5	Today, passenger ships' radios work twenty hours a day.	☐	☐

THE NIGHT THE TITANIC SANK

Look at the following lines from the book. They all happened on the night the *Titanic* sank; match them with the time at which they took place.

So John Phillips began to use the call SOS.

In the radio room, John Phillips sent his call for help again and again. The first reply was from the *Frankfort*.

Stone spoke to Captain Lord on the telephone. 'The ship has sent eight rockets. She is very low in the water.'

Captain Lord jumped up. 'Quick,' he said. 'Get this ship there now. We must help if we can.'

There was a number of very loud bangs. Then the noise stopped. 'That's the last of her.'

The captain said, 'Get the lifeboats ready. Tell the passengers. The ship is sinking.'

The radio officers on the *Californian* finished work.

11.30 ....
12.05 ....
12.18 ....
12.45 ....
2.05   ....
2.20   ....
5.42   ....

B Language Skills

1 WORD STUDY

On page 15 of *The Titanic is Sinking*, Thomas Andrews says, 'Water will fill all the compartments **one by one**.' Match the expressions with **one**, (1–4), with their meanings in the second list.

1 one-to-one ☐ in one direction
2 one-way ☐ unfair
3 one-sided ☐ something made or happening only once
4 one-off ☐ with two people, face to face

Now use the expressions with **one** in the following sentences.

5 They never wanted to see John again, so they gave him a .... ticket to Brazil.
6 The dress was most unusual; it was a .... which was made by Chanel in Paris.
7 The teacher met her student for a .... lesson.
8 Jack's argument was very .... He would not accept that what Katie thought was important too.

2 VERB FORMS

Read this report by one of the survivors of the *Titanic* and fill the gaps using the correct form of the verb.

It's strange – I don't remember¹ (*remember*) much about that night. It ....² (*be*) late and I ....³ (*dance*) to the band with my husband. Everyone ....⁴ (*be*) very happy because we were close to North America.

Suddenly we ....⁵ (*feel*) something against the ship. No one ....⁶ (*know*) what it was and we continued to dance. One of the officers came in soon after and said 'We ....⁷ (*hit*) an iceberg, but it's nothing to worry about.'

'Don't worry, Lucy,' my husband said. 'They ....⁸ (*build*) this ship to last.'

After that I only ....⁹ (*remember*) waiting next to the lifeboats. The back of the ship was very low in the water: the *Titanic* ....¹⁰ (*sink*)! One of the officers ....¹¹ (*tell*) me to get into the lifeboat. 'I ....¹² (*not go*) without my husband,' I said.

'Please - I ....¹³ (*see*) you in New York, when this is all over. I promise.'

In fact I did see my husband in New York - we were lucky. After the ship ....¹⁴ (*sink*) he stayed in the sea for several hours in his life-jacket. A sailor from the *Frankfort* ....¹⁵ (*save*) him.

3 PREPOSITIONS

Fill the gaps in the text below with a preposition from the box. You will need to use some of the prepositions more than once.

| down   of   on   near   onto   in   below |

The sailors started to get the lifeboats ready. There were sixteen boats: eight ....[1] each side. Four were ....[2] the back. And four were nearer the front. They were all made ....[3] wood. There were also four boats made ....[4] cloth.

All the boats together could carry 1178 people. There were 2207 people ....[5] the *Titanic*. 'The *Titanic* cannot sink! She's the biggest ship ....[6] the world!' the passengers thought.

An officer came to tell the captain a few minutes later that the windows were all closed. 'Nobody can get .... [7]!' he said.

'Well, open the windows. Break them but get the passengers .... [8] the boats!'

The captain knew that they only had an hour left. There was a hole about 100 metres long .... [9] the water and the water would soon fill all sixteen compartments.

1502 people went .... [10] with the *Titanic*. It was one of the worst shipping disasters of all time.

THE TITANIC IS SINKING

4 COMPARATIVES AND SUPERLATIVES

Complete the sentences below using one of the adjectives in the box in a comparative or superlative form.

beautiful poor dangerous cold fast big rich ~~strong~~

1 Harland and Wolff used the *strongest* metal they had to build the ship.
2 Lady Pirrie said she wanted the ship to be .... than other ships.
3 Mr Ismay told his friends that he wanted the three ships to be the .... passenger ships in the world.
4 The .... passengers on the *Titanic* were travelling third-class.
5 There were icebergs in the sea near Newfoundland because it is one of the .... areas of sea in the world.
6 Travelling through this part of the sea was .... than travelling from Cherbourg to Ireland because of the icebergs.
7 The *Titanic* was travelling .... than the *Californian*.
8 The .... passengers had large, luxurious cabins on the *Titanic*.

C Activities

WRITING

You are a sailor who was saved from the *Titanic*. You have been asked by the police to write about what happened. The police are trying to find out why so many people went down with the ship and what caused the accident.

Write a report of about 75 words.

DISCUSSION

Many people today go on 'cruises'. These are trips on large, beautiful ships which go from one lovely port to another in the Mediterranean, the Caribbean and other seas. Discuss with a partner whether or not you would like to go on a cruise.

Glossary

bridge
> the place high up at the front of the ship from which it is directed

build
> make (i.e. a house, a boat, a bridge etc.)

cloth
> a type of material made from wool, cotton etc., here the cloth is strong and rough

compartment
> a separate part of something, i.e. train compartment

iceberg
> a large piece of ice found in very cold seas

Lady
> a woman of social importance in Britain, married to a Lord

Let's leave the men to their drinks.
> It was usual for the rich to form two groups after dinner. The men would move to another room to drink alcoholic drinks; the women would drink tea or coffee

life-jacket
> a coat worn by passengers and sailors in emergencies to keep their heads above the surface of the sea

lifeboat
> a small boat carried by a larger boat, used in emergencies to take passengers to safety

Lord
> a man of social importance in Britain, married to a Lady

night clothes
> clothes worn to bed

officer
> a person who has a position of authority on a ship

passenger ship
   a ship carrying mostly people
radio officer
   the person in charge of the radio work
rocket
   something which is sent out as a signal from a ship if there is a problem
shipping line
   a company that has many ships
sink
   go slowly down below the surface of the water
soul
   the non-physical part of a person, where the person's true nature and deepest thoughts are said to be. It is believed to continue existing after the body is dead
We are 41.46 North, 50.14 West.
   Numbers used to tell someone a ship's position on a map of the world

Longman English Library

Series editor: Lewis Jones

A library of graded readers for students of English as a foreign language, and for reluctant native readers. The books are graded in six levels of difficulty.

Structure, vocabulary, idiom and sentence length are all controlled. Level 1 has a basic vocabulary of 300 words and appropriate structures, 2: 600 words, 3: 1000 words, 4: 1500 words, 5: 2000 words and 6: 2500 words. Those titles which are asterisked are accompanied by a cassette.

Level Two

The Canterville Ghost* *Oscar Wilde*
The Prince and the Poor Boy *Mark Twain*
Inspector Holt: The Bridge* *John Tully*
Oliver Twist *Charles Dickens*
The Titanic is Sinking* *K R Cripwell*
Three Sherlock Holmes Adventures* *Sir Arthur Conan Doyle*
Chariots of Fire* *W J Weatherby*
Moonfleet *J Meade Falkner*